Dear Parents:

Congratulations! Your child is taking the first steps on an exciting journey. The destination? Independent reading!

STEP INTO READING® will help your child get there. The program offers five steps to reading success. Each step includes fun stories and colorful art or photographs. In addition to original fiction and books with favorite characters, there are Step into Reading Non-Fiction Readers, Phonics Readers and Boxed Sets, Sticker Readers, and Comic Readers—a complete literacy program with something to interest every child.

Learning to Read, Step by Step!

Ready to Read   Preschool–Kindergarten
• big type and easy words • rhyme and rhythm • picture clues
For children who know the alphabet and are eager to begin reading.

Reading with Help   Preschool–Grade 1
• basic vocabulary • short sentences • simple stories
For children who recognize familiar words and sound out new words with help.

Reading on Your Own   Grades 1–3
• engaging characters • easy-to-follow plots • popular topics
For children who are ready to read on their own.

Reading Paragraphs   Grades 2–3
• challenging vocabulary • short paragraphs • exciting stories
For newly independent readers who read simple sentences with confidence.

Ready for Chapters   Grades 2–4
• chapters • longer paragraphs • full-color art
For children who want to take the plunge into chapter books but still like colorful pictures.

STEP INTO READING® is designed to give every child a successful reading experience. The grade levels are only guides; children will progress through the steps at their own speed, developing confidence in their reading. The F&P Text Level on the back cover serves as another tool to help you choose the right book for your child.

Remember, a lifetime love of reading starts with a single step!

Text copyright © 2020 by Amy Krouse Rosenthal Revocable Trust
Cover art and interior illustrations copyright © 2020 by Brigette Barrager
Written by Candice Ransom
Illustrations by Sue DiCicco

Step into Reading, Random House, and the Random House colophon are registered trademarks of Penguin Random House LLC.

Visit us on the Web!
StepIntoReading.com
rhcbooks.com

Educators and librarians, for a variety of teaching tools, visit us at RHTeachersLibrarians.com

Library of Congress Cataloging-in-Publication Data is available upon request.
ISBN 978-0-593-17802-7 (trade) — ISBN 978-0-593-17803-4 (lib. bdg.) — ISBN 978-0-593-17804-1 (ebook)

Printed in the United States of America
10 9 8 7 6 5 4 3 2 1

This book has been officially leveled by using the F&P Text Level Gradient™ Leveling System.

UNI

Uni the UNICORN

Bakes a Cake

an Amy Krouse Rosenthal book
pictures based on art by Brigette Barrager

Random House 🏠 New York

Uni is thinking of
the little girl.
It feels sad
to miss a friend.

So Uni slides down
a rainbow
to the little girl's house.

"Hi, Uni!" says the little girl.
"Stella and Charlie and I
are baking cakes
for a contest."

Stella puts frosting
on hers.

"I hope my fancy cake
will win," she says.

Charlie takes his cake
out of the oven.
"I hope my chocolate cake
will win," he says.

"I am baking
a different cake,"
says Uni's friend.

The little girl
stirs the batter.
Uni wants to help.
"Don't forget the eggs!"
says Uni.

The little girl
adds the eggs
and stirs.

They pour the batter
into pans.

The pans go
into the oven.

Soon they smell
warm cake.
Ding!
The pans come out
of the oven.

"Oh, no!" the little girl cries.
Her cakes have sunk
in the middle!

"Fill the holes
with frosting," says Uni.
"Good idea,"
says the little girl.

She mixes sugar, butter,
and vanilla.

"Don't forget the milk."
Uni points to
a bottle of milk.

Uni's friend
pours in the milk.
"Oh, no!" she cries.
"Too much!"

Uni's friend pours
frosting on the cake.
It slides down the sides.

"My cake is
a drippy mess,"
the little girl says.

"That's okay," Uni says.
"It's different!"

Ding-dong!

The judge is here.

The judge looks
at Stella's fancy cake.
"Pretty!" he says.

"My cake is
not pretty,"
says Uni's friend.

Next the judge tastes
Charlie's chocolate cake.
"Yummy!" he says.

"My cake will not
taste yummy,"
says Uni's friend.

Uni knows how hard
the little girl worked.
Her cake needs
a chance!

No one sees
Uni's horn tap
the little girl's cake,
once, twice.

The judge looks at
the cake.
It glows with
rainbow sparkles!
"Oh!" the little girl says.

The judge cuts

a slice to taste.

It looks like
a rainbow inside!
"Different,"
says the judge.

"It is hard to choose,"
he says.
"But I love the
chocolate cake."
He puts a ribbon
next to Charlie's cake.

Uni feels sad.

The little girl hugs Uni.

"Thank you!" she says.
"You made my cake
really different!"

"But it did not win,"
says Uni.
"It's okay,"
says the little girl.

"We had fun," she says.
"Best friends help
each other."

"And best friends
eat cake together!"
says Uni.